ESCAPE!

PAULINE CARTWRIGHT

ILLUSTRATED BY
LORENZO VAN DER LINGEN

Learning Media

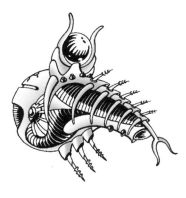

STARSHIP ASTRA

SHUTTLE 2

STARSHIP ASTRA was in trouble. Their engine was down to half power. They needed trillium metal to fix it. They had stopped near a strange, dark planet. Zimm and Tarek had taken a shuttle to explore the planet, and to look for the metal they needed.

ZIMM

TAREK

1.

THE DARK PLANET

The shuttle looked tiny next to the dark planet. On board, Zimm and Tarek had waited for two hours. They called the *Astra*.

"Captain, our probe hasn't come back. Something must have happened. We're going down to find it."

"OK. But keep in touch," said Captain Voss. "We need that trillium for the engine."

The shuttle flew close to the planet.
It was dusty and rocky, with no plants
growing.

"It looks safe," said Tarek.

"I'll send down a scanner to make sure
everything's OK," said Zimm.

They watched the scanner. Before it got to the surface, it exploded.

"Wow!" cried Zimm. "What happened?"

2.
THE FORCE FIELD

Zimm fired two more scanners, and there were two more explosions.

"I believe that is what happened to our probe," said Tarek. "We are not alone here."

Zimm sent out another scanner.
It floated down and landed safely.

"That is good," said Tarek. "The force
field stops by the rocks over there."

"So someone's down there!" said Zimm.
"Why don't they want us to land?
Who are they?"

"We need to find out," said Tarek.
"We can fly to the side of the force field
and creep in."

The shuttle swooped low. Once they had landed, Zimm and Tarek could not talk to the crew on the *Astra*. The force field stopped their radio from working. They were on their own.

Zimm hid the shuttle behind some rocks. "Something strange is going on," she said. "I don't know who *or what* is out there. We have to keep the shuttle a secret!"

3.
TRILLIUM

Zimm and Tarek put on their space gear and left the shuttle. Outside, the planet was cold and dusty.

"There's no wind," said Zimm.
"So where is all this dust coming from?"
They walked away from the shuttle and
looked around for trillium rock.

"I'd hate to stay here forever,"
said Zimm.

"I like it. It is just like home,"
said Tarek.

They put rock samples into their bags
and looked out for danger. Someone,
somewhere on this planet,
had made that
force field.

At the top of a hill, Zimm stopped suddenly and waved at Tarek. "Look! Down there!" she whispered. "What on earth are they?"

"They are Andrals," said Tarek. "They are a long way from their home planet."

Zimm and Tarek slowly moved closer.
"What are they doing?" asked Zimm.
"Can you see what they're doing,
Tarek?"

"I believe they are digging trillium rock,"
said Tarek. "And that machine is making
it into trillium metal. That is where the
dust is coming from."

"Our trillium," gurgled a voice.

4.
THE ANDRALS

Behind them stood three Andrals. Their eyes made Zimm shiver. Tarek had been to the planet Andral. The people there had been friendly, but these Andrals were not smiling.

"We mean no harm," said Tarek.
"We come as friends."

"How did you enter?" asked one.

"There is a gap in your force field,"
said Tarek. "A shuttle dropped us off."

Zimm tried not to look surprised.
She knew they had to keep the hidden
shuttle a secret.

"There is a lot of trillium here,"
said Zimm.

One of the Andrals looked angry.
"Ours! Our trillium!" he gurgled. "Our
planet is poor. We have to sell trillium
to buy food and fuel for Andral."

"Yes," said Tarek. "Your trillium. We
have come to look for a missing probe."

"It may have hit the force field," said
another Andral. "Now, come with us."

They took Zimm and Tarek down to the
Andral camp.

Tarek and Zimm were amazed at the
trillium in the rock. They needed to get
some of that metal on to their shuttle.

5.
NO GUNS

The Andral leader was called Quod. He asked Zimm and Tarek a lot of questions. Tarek told him a shuttle was coming to get them in twelve hours.

"Why do you carry guns?" asked Quod.

"They are not guns," said Tarek. "They are freeze-beams. They let us escape without hurting anyone."

"Well," gurgled Quod, "if you wish to look for your probe, you will have to leave the freeze-beams with us. Now, we have work to do." He waved his arms around. "Look, but touch *nothing*."

"I do not think they want to harm us," said Tarek. "But we have to be careful."

They walked around and watched the Andrals working. There was trillium everywhere. They could see Quod and the others talking. Quod looked angry. Zimm and Tarek crept behind a rock to listen.

"The shuttle must not land."

"But they say they are friends."

"But they may tell others …."

"We must shut down the force field and fix it now!" said Quod.

Zimm and Tarek walked over to the camp. They tried not to look scared.

"I thought we were safe!" whispered Zimm. "They want to keep us here!"

"And we have to get some trillium for the *Astra's* engine," said Tarek. "One block is all we need."

"They have our freeze-beams," said Tarek. "If they know how to work them, they can stop us easily. We have to go now, before they fix the force field."

"Fly right over their heads?" Zimm was worried.

"Would you rather stay here forever?" asked Tarek.

"No! Let's go!" said Zimm. They walked past the machine and looked at the Andrals working.

"Now!" whispered Tarek.

They turned around and walked quietly and quickly away.

6.

ESCAPE

How much further could it be? They wanted to start running. Then, at last, they reached the rocks.

Their hearts were beating fast as they climbed aboard the shuttle.

When the shuttle engine started, they saw Andrals on the top of a hill beside them.

"We're just in time," said Zimm. "They were checking up on us!"

The ship gathered power. "Can you fly over the camp?" said Tarek. "We have to beam up a block of trillium."

"They could stop us with our freeze-beams," said Zimm. "We have to go fast."

The shuttle zoomed low over the camp. Tarek beamed up a block of trillium. "We will send them payment from the *Astra*," he said.

"They're using the freeze-beams," yelled
Zimm. "We're too low."

"And too fast, I hope," said Tarek.

7.
"WE'RE OUT!"

Suddenly, they heard a voice. "*Astra* calling shuttle. Come in, shuttle …."

Zimm gave a shout: "We're out! We're out! The force field is still shut down!" She took the shuttle higher far above the Andrals. They were safe.

"Shuttle calling *Astra*," Tarek replied. "We are leaving the planet."

"And I have a present for you, Captain Voss," said Zimm. She patted the block of trillium by her seat.

"Trillium is very useful," said Tarek.

"Yes, but I don't want to spend my life digging it up for someone else," said Zimm.

"I have to agree," said Tarek. "Set a course for the *Astra*."

Zimm smiled. "Shuttle to *Astra*," she called. "Look out! We're coming in!"